MW01120934

Rosie's Birthday Rat

A Yearling First Choice Chapter Book

Rosie's Birthday Rat

Linda Glaser

illustrated by
Nancy Poydar

To Laurel, who showed me the way,
and to Midnight, who opened my heart to rats.
—L.G.

To Jennifer, who will long remember her friend Ruth the rat.
—N.P.

Published by
Bantam Doubleday Dell Publishing Group, Inc.
1540 Broadway
New York, New York 10036

Library of Congress Cataloging-in-Publication Data
The hardback of this title is cataloged as follows:
Glaser, Linda.
Rosie's birthday rat / written by Linda Glaser ; illustrated by Nancy Poydar.
p.   cm.
"A Yearling First Choice Chapter Book."
Summary: Rosie's mother reluctantly agrees to get her a rat for her birthday, but
it takes Rosie a while to convince her mother that she made the right decision.
ISBN 0-385-32172-4 (alk. paper). — ISBN 0-440-41113-0 (pbk. : alk. paper)
[1. Rats as pets—Fiction.   2. Pets—Fiction.   3. Mothers and daughters—
Fiction.]   I. Poydar, Nancy, ill.   II. Title.
PZ7.G48047Ro   1996
[Fic]—dc20   95-21363   CIP   AC

Hardcover: The trademark Delacorte Press® is registered in the U.S. Patent and
Trademark Office and in other countries.
Paperback: The trademark Yearling® is registered in the U.S. Patent and
Trademark Office and in other countries.

The text of this book is set in 17-point Baskerville.
Manufactured in the United States of America
June 1996
10   9   8   7   6   5   4   3   2   1

Contents

1.
Rosie Wants a Rat

"I want a rat for my birthday,"
Rosie told her mom.
"Sorry," said her mom.
"You can have a bird or a dog."

Rosie frowned. "I want a rat."

Her mom shivered.

"Rats give me the creeps.

Why do you want one?"

"Because," said Rosie.

"We had a rat in my kindergarten.

We had a rat in my first grade.

Now we have a rat in my second grade.

I know them the best.

I like them the best.

I've grown up with rats!"

"But rats are ugly rodents," said her mom.

"What about something else?"

"No," said Rosie. "I only want a rat."

"What about Max, our cat?"

asked her mom.

Rosie shrugged and said,

"He's *your* cat. *I* want a rat."

"But cats don't like rats,"
said her mom.

"We'll keep them apart," said Rosie.

"Rats are wild," said her mom.

"Pet rats are not wild," said Rosie.

"Pet rats are sweet."

"I don't want a rat in our house,"
said her mom.

"But I'll feed it. I'll clean its cage.

I'll play with it. I'll love it.

That's what I want for my birthday.

Nothing else." Rosie folded her arms.

Her mom thought for a long time.

Finally she said,

"I can't believe we're getting a rat."

10

Rosie jumped in the air.

"Thank you, Mom!"

"I hope you won't be sorry,"
said her mom.

"I won't!" said Rosie.

"I'm already sorry!" said her mom.

Rosie hugged her tight. "You won't be.
Just wait and see."

2.
At the Snake Store

The next day Rosie and her mom
went to the East Bay Snake Store.
A clerk came over.

His hair was short on top
and long down the back.
He had big black boots
and a snake tattoo on his arm.
"Hi there!"
His voice was low and raspy.
"Can I help you?" he asked.

Rosie wasn't so sure.
"We're looking for baby rats,"
she said.
"Here they are,"
said the clerk.
He showed them a box.

There were small, furry bodies
squirming around.

"You need some for snake food?"
asked the clerk.

"Oh no!" Rosie exclaimed.

"I want one for a pet."

"No problem," said the clerk.

"We sell them for that, too."

Rosie nodded. "I know.

My teacher bought one here.
Rats are the best pets.

They're smart and friendly."

Rosie lifted one out of the box.

It felt soft and warm.

She stroked it on the head.

It was black as a night sky.

Its belly was white like a cloud.

It had a white V on its forehead.

"If you're gentle with them,

they'll be gentle with you,"

she explained.

"Oh yeah?" asked the clerk.

He petted the rat with his finger.

"They need a lot of love,"

Rosie told him.

"Here. Let me have it for a second,"

said the clerk.

He took a good look.
"She *is* cute," he said.
Then he held the rat close
and kissed it—right on the nose!
"Oh my!" exclaimed Rosie's mom.

He shrugged. "Hey, it's a nice rat."

He sounded as if *he* wanted it.

"Her name is Midnight," said Rosie.

"She's *my* rat.

And *I'm* taking her home."

"I still can't believe it,"

said her mom.

"A rat in our house!"

She half-smiled.

"Well, happy birthday, Rosie!"

Rosie grinned.

"I'm *so* happy. And you will be, too!"

3.
Midnight's Tail

On the car ride home,

Midnight stayed in a box on Rosie's lap.

"I want to hold her so bad!" said Rosie.

"Please wait!" said her mom.

Rosie could hardly wait.

But she had to. Finally they got home.

Rosie took the box into her room.

She shut the door

so Max the cat wouldn't get in.

Then she opened the box

and lifted Midnight out.

Midnight was soft and warm.

She settled into Rosie's hands

as if she belonged there.

She had tiny pink toes, bright black eyes,
and a sweet pink nose.

"I love you," Rosie whispered.

"I saved your life."

Midnight scurried up Rosie's arm
and onto her shoulder.

Rosie's mom came in.

Max the cat tried to slip in, too.

But Rosie's mom quickly shut the door.

She looked at Midnight and shivered.

"That tail gives me the creeps!"

Rosie covered Midnight's tail.

"Now is she cute?" Rosie asked.

"Well, yes," said her mom.

"As long as you hide that tail."

"Try holding her, Mom," said Rosie.

"She's *so* sweet."

Her mom shuddered. "No thanks.

She's not *that* sweet.

But *you* are."

She kissed Rosie on the cheek.

Rosie wiped it off with her sleeve.

She stroked Midnight

from the top of her head

to the tip of her tail.

"Look!" said Rosie.

"She's kissing me."

"You like *rat* kisses

but not *my* kisses?"

her mom teased.

"You should feel them," said Rosie.

Midnight licked some more.

Tiny pink licks.

Then she nestled in Rosie's hands,

curled into a ball, and fell asleep.

"Welcome home," Rosie whispered.

And she held her

and held her

and held her.

4.
The Best
Birthday Present

Rosie sat with Midnight in her lap.
"Here's some birthday cake."
She served the cake on a toy plate.

Midnight took the cake
in her tiny pink fingers.
She ate and ate,
and licked and licked.
"You're the best birthday present
in the world," said Rosie.
"I hope you like your new home."
She put Midnight into her cage.

27

But it didn't look cozy.

So Rosie put a little paper bag upstairs.

Midnight scurried in and out.

Then Rosie put an old washcloth down.

It looked like a welcome mat.

Midnight sat on the mat

and washed her face.

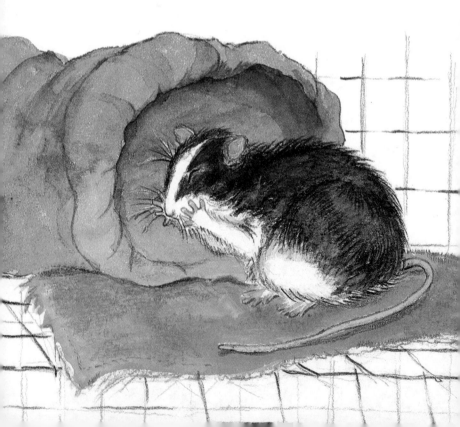

Then Midnight ran downstairs,
twitching her little pink nose.
Rosie tore tissue paper into long strips.
She gave a piece to Midnight.
Midnight held it in her mouth and
scampered back upstairs.
The tissue waved behind her
like a streamer.
She stuffed it into her bag
and ran down for more.

After a while Rosie's mom came in.

"What a mess!" said her mom.

"It looks like a rat's nest in there."

Rosie giggled. "It *is* a rat's nest, Mom!

I want to shrink down

and go inside."

"Please keep the cage door shut tight,"

said her mom.

"I don't want a rat's nest
anywhere else in our house."
"I wish you liked Midnight," said Rosie.
She cut out a tiny red paper heart.
Midnight took it gently in her mouth.
She scampered into her bag
and put Rosie's heart deep inside.
Such a sweet rat!
Why didn't her mom see that?

5.
Midnight's Grandma

That evening
Rosie held Midnight up to her face
and looked in the mirror.
"Midnight looks just like me,"
she told her mom. "See?"

"No, I don't see," said her mom.
"We both have the same dark eyes,"
said Rosie.
"And my hair is dark like hers.
And it parts in the middle
and makes a V on my forehead
just like Midnight's."

"And you both have two big front teeth
and twitchy noses," her mom joked.
"We do."
Rosie wiggled her nose
and showed her big front teeth.
"She looks like me
because I'm her mom.
And that makes you . . . her grandma!"
Her mom laughed. Rosie smiled.
"*You* know what grandmas do."

She held Midnight out to her mom.

"Please try?"

"She *is* pretty," said her mom.

"Be brave. Hold her. Please, Mom?"

"Oh, all right." She cupped her hands.

Rosie placed Midnight in them.

"Try petting her," said Rosie.

"Hmm." Her mom smiled. "She *is* soft."

"See?" said Rosie. "Isn't she sweet?"

"Except for the tail," said her mom.

Midnight poked under her sleeve
and crawled inside.

"She's getting cozy," said Rosie.

"She's going up my arm!"
cried Rosie's mom.

"Get her out!"

She shook and wiggled.

Rosie tried not to giggle.

"Hold still, Mom!"

"Do something!" shouted her mom.

"Help! She's under my blouse!"

Her eyes bugged out.

Rosie burst out laughing.

"Oh *no*!" her mom shrieked.

"She's crawling around in there!"

Her mom pointed to her chest.

"Get her, Rosie. And stop laughing!"

Rosie couldn't stop laughing.

"Here, Midnight!" Rosie called.

A little bump moved up her mom's blouse.

Suddenly Midnight's head poked out from her mom's collar.

Rosie grabbed her.

"Midnight! Good girl!

You came when I called!

Oh, you poor thing. You were scared."

"*I* was scared, too!" said her mom.

"It will be better next time," said Rosie.

"There won't be a next time,"

said her mom.

"Yes, there will," said Rosie.

"*You* said she was sweet.

You like her. I can tell."

6.
Midnight Is Missing

The next morning
Rosie rushed over to see Midnight.
Oh no! The cage door was open.
She must have forgotten to close it.
Midnight was gone!

Rosie looked on the floor,

under the bed, in the closet.

Midnight wasn't anywhere.

The bedroom door was open!

Midnight must be loose in the house.

What if Max the cat found her?

Rosie burst into tears.

"Rosie, come quick," called her mom.

Rosie ran into the kitchen.

Her mom was on her hands and knees,
staring behind the fridge.

Rosie ran over.

Midnight's pink nose poked out.

"Oh, Mom! You found her!"

"She won't come out," said her mom.

"Yeow!" Max the cat raced in—
right to the fridge.
"Oh no!" Rosie gasped.
She scooped up the cat
and held him tight.
"Don't move, Mom," said Rosie.

She grabbed a cracker.

"Here. Lead Midnight out with this."

Her mom held the cracker.

"Here, Midnight!" her mom called.

Midnight poked out her nose,

then one tiny pink paw, then another.

The cat wiggled in Rosie's arms.

"Quick, Mom! Grab Midnight!"

"Oh, I *can't*!" said her mom.

"Yes, you *can*!" said Rosie firmly.

"Be brave!"

The cat wriggled this way and that.

"Please, Mom, just do it!"

SWISH!

Rosie's mom scooped up Midnight.

"I did it!" she shouted.

"You were great, Mom," said Rosie.

"Meow!" whined Max.

Rosie rushed outside with the cat.

When she came back,

her mom was feeding Midnight.

"Rosie, look how she holds the cracker

in her tiny hands—just like a person!"

"She *is* a person," said Rosie.

"A rat person."

Her mom held Midnight close.

"Nice rat person."

Smooch! Right on the nose!

But not Midnight's nose. Rosie's nose!

Rosie didn't wipe it off.

She hugged her mom.
"Nice grandma!"

Linda Glaser has written several books for children, including another early reader, *Keep Your Socks on, Albert!* She lives in Minnesota.

Nancy Poydar has illustrated many books for children and wrote and illustrated *Busy Bea.* She lives in Massachusetts.